Copy Cat

For Emma Nash,

who loves to draw

First U.S. edition 2018

Library of Congress Catalog Card Number pending
ISBN 978-0-7636-9935-2

18 19 20 21 22 23 WKT 10 9 8 7 6 5 4 3 2 1

Printed in Shenzhen, Guangdong, China

This book was typeset in Century Gothic.
The illustrations were created digitally.

Nosy Crow
an imprint of
Candlewick Press
99 Dover Street
Somerville, Massachusetts 02144

www.nosycrow.com
www.candlewick.com

Copy Cat

Ali Pye

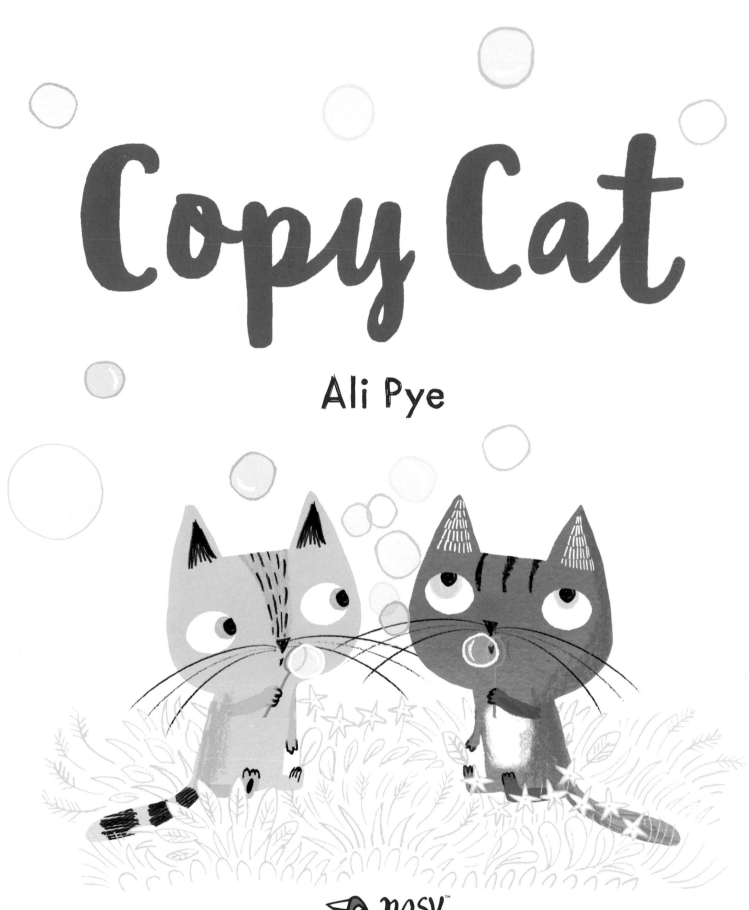

nosy crow

An imprint of Candlewick Press

Bella wanted to be **just** like Anna.

Whatever Anna played . . .

Bella wanted to play, too.

When Anna played ballerina . . .

And when Anna played pirate . . .

Bella wanted to play ballerina, too,
just like Anna.

Bella wanted to play pirate, too,
just like Anna.

So when Anna played princess . . .

of course Bella wanted to be
a princess, too, **just** like Anna.

But there was only

one crown!

Anna was **mad.**

"Bella!" she said.
"You are such a copy cat!
Stop copying me!
I'm the princess. And it's my crown!"

And off Anna went, all huffy-puffy,
to play princess by herself.

What am I going to do now?
thought Bella.

There was **no one** to play with,
no one to copy.
She'd have to play all by herself.

After a while, Bella got a jump rope
out of the toy box. At first she got
all tangled up, but then she
unwound herself and
practiced
and **practiced**
and **practiced** . . .

until she was jumping
so fast, she didn't notice that
Chloe was watching.

"You're good at jumping rope, Bella," said Chloe. "I wish I could do that, too."

"It's easy!" said Bella. "Just **copy** me!"

So they found a jump rope for Chloe, and Bella
slowed down so that Chloe could copy her.
And Chloe **practiced**

and **practiced**

and **practiced** . . .

until she could jump rope, too, **just** like Bella.

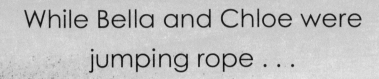

While Bella and Chloe were
jumping rope . . .

Anna was being a huffy-puffy
princess all by herself.

But it was **no fun**
playing princess alone,

so she went to find Bella.

She found Bella **and** Chloe,
jumping rope together.

"I wish I could do that, too," said Anna,
forgetting to be huffy-puffy.

"It's easy!" said Bella and Chloe. "Just **copy** us!"
And they found a jump rope for Anna so she
could copy them.

Anna **practiced** and **practiced** and **practiced**
until she could jump rope **just** like Bella and Chloe.
Then Chloe had an idea.

They found one long rope . . .

and they **all** jumped **together!**

Then they all played
ballerina-pirate-princesses . . .

together.

Sometimes they still liked to copy one another . . .

but sometimes they didn't copy anyone at all.

At least, not until they met . . .

DOTTY!